Writers

BARRY GIFFORD

SEVEN STORIES

NEW YORK • OAKLAND

A SEVEN STORIES PRESS FIRST EDITION

"Spring Training at the Finca Vigía" was published in the magazine *Zyzzyva* (San Francisco) No. 93, in the Winter 2011 issue.

"After Words" ("Palabras después") was published in the magazine *Nexos* (Mexico City) in the January 2015 issue.

"The Last Words of Arthur Rimbaud" was originally published in a limited edition by the Bancroft Library Press (University of California, Berkeley, 1998).

Seven Stories Press
140 Watts Street
New York, NY 10013
sevenstories.com

Library of Congress Cataloging-in-Publication Data

Gifford, Barry, 1946-
[Short stories. Selections]
Writers / Barry Gifford. -- Seven Stories Press First edition.
    pages   cm
ISBN 978-1-60980-649-1 (hardback)
1. Authors--Fiction. I. Title.
PS3557.I283A6 2015
813'.54--dc23

                          2015006307

Printed in the United States of America

9 8 7 6 5 4 3 2 1

FOR DAN

AUTHOR'S NOTE

These pieces are intended to be read as stories as well as performed as plays. They are portraits of writers in wholly imaginary or relatively realistic moments in their lives. I've taken liberties, certainly, with what in several cases has passed for biographical information. The facts are to be found in what they wrote.

—B.G.

CONTENTS

~

Writers

SPRING TRAINING
AT THE FINCA VIGÍA

Ernest Hemingway, 1941

CAST OF CHARACTERS

ERNEST HEMINGWAY, American writer
HUGH CASEY and KIRBY HIGBE, pitchers for the Brooklyn
    Dodgers
MARTHA GELLHORN, Hemingway's wife, also a writer
MANUEL, Hemingway's right hand man
TWO MEN in the darkness

SETTINGS

The Finca Vigía, the home of Ernest Hemingway and Martha
Gellhorn, outside Havana, Cuba, in 1941.

The Floridita, a bar in Havana.

PRODUCTION NOTES

The time of year is early spring. The Brooklyn Dodgers baseball
team is in training for the upcoming major league season and
two of their players, pitchers Hugh Casey and Kirby Higbe, have
become companions of the forty-two-year-old author of *The Sun
Also Rises* and *A Farewell to Arms*, among other books.

SCENE ONE

It is just after ten thirty p.m. when CASEY and HIGBE, led by HEMINGWAY, storm into the house through the front porch door and mill about in the livingroom like lions or tigers driven by the lash of a whip into a cage. Each of them stalks the room warily for a long time, as if they—even Ernest— had never been in it before. They are all more than slightly inebriated.

CASEY

So this is your domain, hey, Ernie? Where you do your drinking.

HIGBE

Call him Ernest, Case. He told us he don't like people callin' him Ernie.

HEMINGWAY

Wherever I am is where I drink. I'm here now.

HIGBE

So are we. We're all three of us here in Cuba.

CASEY

That's right. Higbe's right. What're you gonna do about it, Ernesto?

HEMINGWAY

Might I offer you gentleman a libation?

HIGBE

I thought there was only Cuban women in Cuba.

HEMINGWAY

What's he talkin' about?

CASEY

What're you talkin' about, Ernesto?

HEMINGWAY

I'm offering you bums a beverage.

CASEY

Hell, yes, Hem, we'll take you up on that offer.

HIGBE

Up and up!

HEMINGWAY goes to his wet bar and pours whiskey into glasses for each of them, hands out the drinks

HEMINGWAY

The regulars at the Havana Gun and Country Club surely appreciate your patronage, boys, but I'm not certain they've got enough doves to last you until the end of spring training.

HIGBE

Us country boys are sure as shit some sharpshootin' sons of bitches, you bet.

HEMINGWAY

Hig, I wish I had eagle eyes like you, but I inherited my eyes from my mother. I would've been better off having had an eagle for a mother than the one I have. Her character is as fucked up as her eyesight.

> *HIGBE and CASEY can sense HEM-INGWAY's mood shift at the mention of his mother. They all drink harder.*

HEMINGWAY

Come on, Case, let's put on the gloves.

> *HEMINGWAY takes down two pairs of boxing gloves hanging by their laces from a hook in one corner of the room, tosses a pair to CASEY. As the men are pulling on and lacing up the gloves, assisted by HIGBE, Hemingway's wife, MARTHA GELLHORN, enters. She's a dirty blonde, Barbara Stanwyck type, tough and sassy,*

not terrifically beautiful but attractive and smarter than the men, including her husband, who knows this and hates her because of it. She swiftly and accurately appraises the scene.

GELLHORN

Good evening, children. I'll be damned if I can't hear the third sheet fluttering in the wind.

CASEY

Evenin', Missus Hemingway.

HIGBE

Evenin', missus.

HEMINGWAY

You can dispense with the formality, boys. Señorita Gellhorn don't cotton to the marital terminology. Martha, my esteemed opponent is none other than Mr. Hugh Casey, presently a pitcher for the Brooklyn Dodgers. Serving as second for both of us is Mr. Kirby Higbe, also of the Brooklyn team, and noted author of what has been appropriately dubbed the high, hard one.

HIGBE

Don't listen to him, missus—I mean ma'am. I ain't no author. I'm a pitcher, like Case. It's what they call my numero uno.

GELLHORN

Your Spanish is very good, Mr. Higbe. But don't worry, I listened to Mr. Hemingstein once, and that was enough.

CASEY

I know what you mean. Ol' Ern knows how to convince people in a hurry.

HEMINGWAY

Cut the crap, Case. Hig, get us out of the clinches and keep the furniture out of our way.

GELLHORN

Pardon my asking, Mr. Casey, but aren't you in training?

CASEY

You know, ma'am, I always pitch better when I have a few the night before. It always gives me a guilty feeling out there, and I bear down a little harder.

HIGBE

That's right. Our general manager, Mr. MacPhail, once asked Case with a month to go in the season if he could hold out and Case told him, Larry, if there's enough whiskey left, I can make it.

> *HEMINGWAY and CASEY begin boxing. GELLHORN leaves the room. The two men hit each other hard and often. HIGBE scurries around in a futile attempt to preserve lamps, chairs and other stationary items.*
>
> *Later. HEMINGWAY and CASEY, exhausted, drop into armchairs. HIGBE unties their gloves and pulls them off.*

HEMINGWAY

How many times you go down, Case?

CASEY

I don't know. Six or seven, I guess.

HEMINGWAY

You count the knockdowns, Hig?

HIGBE

Yeah, six, seven maybe if it weren't for him landin' on the settee.

HEMINGWAY

Never for more than a second or two. You knocked me down twice, Case. You're a tough fella.

HIGBE

I'll say he's tough, Ernest. One day last September the Cardinals was poundin' Hughie pretty good and Durocher stomps out to the mound to get him. Had me warmin' up. I'm ready to go, about to leave the bullpen, but I see Case and Leo jawin' for a while, then Leo walks back to the dugout. I never saw so many batters hit the dirt as after that. Case musta hit eight or nine.

CASEY

Ten.

HIGBE

They beat us nine to one. Back at the hotel, I asked Case why Leo left him in. Tell Hem what you told me, Hughie.

It looked like the game was lost anyway, so I asked Leo to leave me in and I would teach those Cardinal hitters a lesson they'd never forget. Told Durocher I'd put stitchmarks on their sides and backs so they wouldn't dare dig in against me again. But my fastball ain't nothin' compared to Kirby's. His heater sounds like a freight train comin' in.

HEMINGWAY

I heard a sound like that once. It was on the front in the war. When I woke up, two Italian soldiers were dead and a third was screaming. I picked him up and carried him back to a medical tent while the Jerries kept firing their machine guns. I got hit in the ankle and then the knee, but I managed to crawl the last ten yards to the tent. When I got there the third soldier was dead and my kneecap was blown off. The doctors fished out a hundred or more pieces of shrapnel from my leg. Three months later, I limped out of the hospital with a metal kneecap. Couldn't walk without a cane for almost a year.

HIGBE

Me'n Case put a few boys in the hospital, usually from throwin' the spitter, which ain't easy to control, but even we can't compete with a machine gun.

CASEY

You win, Ernesto. Let's drink to it.

> *HEMINGWAY rises with difficulty, goes over to the bar, opens a new bottle, puts out three clean glasses, and pours.*

HEMINGWAY

Fire when ready, gentlemen.

∾

SCENE TWO

Midnight at the Finca Vigía. HEM-INGWAY stands on the front porch of the house wearing only a pair of khaki shorts and sandals. He is holding a shotgun, which he points into the darkness.

HEMINGWAY

Come on, you cowards! Come into the light where I can knock you on your asses. I've shot and killed leopards in less light by just the glint off the cinder in their eyes.

GELLHORN comes out onto the porch wearing a nightgown and slippers.

GELLHORN

What is it, Ernest? Who are you going to shoot?

HEMINGWAY

Thieves in the night, Martha. Gutless creeps who call themselves rebels to justify stealing from people who've worked goddamn hard to get what they have.

GELLHORN

I didn't hear anything.

HEMINGWAY

They don't have the nerve of jackals. You can't hear 'em or see 'em until you feel their hands in your pockets. Some terrorists, these boys. Afraid of the trip wires.

GELLHORN

What trip wires?

HEMINGWAY

Shhh. I haven't installed them yet. Manuel is bringing the explosives tomorrow from Matanzas. Had the ordnance shipped from the Dominican.

GELLHORN

I won't allow it, Ernest. Someone will get hurt.

GELLHORN

You're right about that, sister.

GELLHORN

I mean you and your borracho buddies. What'll the owner of the Dodgers say when his star pitcher comes back to Brooklyn in pieces?

HEMINGWAY

Won't happen, woman. It's these sneaking phony mothergrabbers who'll lose the balls they wish they'd had in the first place.

GELLHORN

You always say you're for the rebels.

HEMINGWAY

It's Batista I'm against, not the rebels I'm for.

*GELLHORN disappears for a moment,
then reappears on the porch holding a large
flashlight, which she shines into the blackness.*

GELLHORN

I guess you've scared them away, Ernest, you and your popgun.

HEMINGWAY

I was shooting the tails off lizards at twenty yards up in
Michigan when I was eight years old while you were at Miss
Prisspussy's School in St. Louis learning which fork to use first.

GELLHORN

(turns off the flashlight)

I hadn't yet been born when those lizards lost their tails. Don't
they grow back, anyway?

HEMINGWAY

Put that torch on again.

GELLHORN

I'm going back to bed. Don't wound the dogs or shoot the tails
off any of the cats.

*GELLHORN re-enters the house. HEM-
INGWAY stands alone on the porch, still
pointing the shotgun into the night. Finally*

he picks it up and goes inside. The porch light goes off. A few moments later, the door opens again, very slowly, and HEMINGWAY silently re-takes his position with his weapon. There is a rustling sound; some person or animal is moving in the darkness. HEMINGWAY raises his shotgun and fires one barrel, then the second. After the ringing sound of the firings ends, there is complete silence. HEMINGWAY turns and goes back into the house.

TWO MEN appear, one on either side of the porch. They move toward one another and meet just below the place where HEMINGWAY had been standing. Both have revolvers in their hands. Slowly they slink away from the house and disappear into the darkness.

∽

SCENE THREE

Inside the Floridita, a bar in Havana. HEMINGWAY is seated on a stool in a corner, a daiquiri on the bar in front of him. Seated on stools near Hemingway are CASEY and HIGBE and MANUEL, a Cuban. CASEY and HIGBE are drinking daiquiris. On the bar in front of MANUEL is a small glass of rum.

CASEY

But why would they come after you, Ernest?

HIGBE

Yeah, especially if you're backin' 'em.

HEMINGWAY

They killed one of my dogs. It's Cuba for the Cubans. We Americanos aren't long for this place.

HIGBE

You're too famous to kill.

HEMINGWAY

But not too famous to die. There's a difference.

CASEY

What do you think, Manuel? Would they kill Ernesto?

MANUEL

Sí, if they think it is in the interest to advance the revolution.

HIGBE

They wouldn't shoot an American ballplayer, though, would they?

HEMINGWAY

A Yankee, maybe, but not a Dodger. All of them laugh. The four men drink.

MANUEL

Señor Hugh, who is the best hitter you have ever faced?

HIGBE

Yeah, Hughie, who?

CASEY

Ducky Medwick, no doubt about it. Up, down, in, out, don't matter. Ducky swings, bang, it's a double up against the wall.

HEMINGWAY

My wife's from St. Louis, too.

HIGBE

She a Cardinal fan?

HEMINGWAY

She likes the color red. She even thought she was one once.

CASEY

What, a Cardinal?

HEMINGWAY

No, a Red.

(He stands.)

Manuel and I have to be goin', boys. We've got some ordnance to unload in Matanzas.

HIGBE

When I was in the army, my CO said I wasn't too good takin' orders.

CASEY

Okay, Ernesto, will we be seein' you later?

Come out to the house tomorrow night. I'll have something to show you.

HEMINGWAY and MANUEL exit the Floridita.

HIGBE

Do you really think them rebels would kill Ernest, Hughie?

CASEY

How do I know, Hig? I can't even figure a way to get Ducky Medwick out.

HIGBE

You ain't alone.

(They tap their glasses and drink.)

~

SCENE FOUR

The next night. HEMINGWAY, HIGBE, CASEY and MANUEL are all seated on the porch of Ernest and Martha's house. They are drinking. A shotgun is stood on end against Hemingway's chair.

HEMINGWAY

The way it works is someone trips over the wire, the lights come on and the explosive planted closest to where the wire was tripped is set off.

CASEY

What if it's an animal? Or a friend don't know the wire's there?

HEMINGWAY

There's always collateral damage in a war, Case.

> *GELLHORN comes out of the house onto the porch.*

CASEY AND HIGBE

Evenin', Missus Hemingway.

GELLHORN

Mister Casey, my husband tells me you have trouble pitching to Ducky Medwick.

CASEY

Yes, ma'am. He pretty much owns me.

GELLHORN

I'm from St. Louis.

CASEY

Yes, ma'am, we know. A great baseball town.

GELLHORN

I've had the opportunity to study Mr. Medwick's batting method. It seems to me that he has a hard time laying off an inside pitch just above the hands, especially when he's deep in the count.

HIGBE

Shoot, Case, she might could have somethin' there.

CASEY

I'll keep that in mind, Missus H. I appreciate the advice.

GELLHORN

Ernest, you and your posse please remember to pick up the body parts before you call it a night. I don't want to have to clean up after you in the morning. Buenos noches, gentlemen.

GELLHORN goes inside.

CASEY AND HIGBE

Good night, ma'am.

CASEY

She's all right, Ernest.

HIGBE

You done good marryin' her, I think, Ernesto. Inside above the hands. That's what Mr. Rickey would call a keen observation.

HEMINGWAY

I'm beginning to think you fellows have had far too little experience with women.

> *CASEY starts to speak but HEMINGWAY*
> *raises his hand.*

HEMINGWAY (CONT'D)

Shh. I heard something.

> (He stands and picks up the shotgun.)

You think it horrible that lust and rage
Should dance attendance upon my old age;
They were not such a plague when I was young;
What else have I to spur me into song?

CASEY

Hell, Ern, you ain't but forty-two. That ain't old.

> *HEMINGWAY sits down again, holding*
> *the shotgun across his lap.*

HEMINGWAY

Mr. Yeats understood his own words, gentlemen. Age is a state of mind.

HIGBE

Yeah, when my arm goes dead I'm goin' back to the state of Arkansas and stay put. Just enjoy the peace and quiet.

HEMINGWAY

I envy you, Higbe, truly I do. For many of us, a peaceful denouement is not in the cards.

There is a loud CLICK, followed by a few seconds of silence, then a small explosion. A man shouts and then there is the sound of running.

CASEY

I think maybe you scored, Ernest.

HEMINGWAY

Manuel, take a look.

MANUEL leaves the porch and disappears into the darkness. There are thirty seconds of silence.

MANUEL
(from the darkness)

Hay nada, Ernesto. He run away.

HEMINGWAY

It's okay. The bastards know we mean business now.

GELLHORN comes back out onto the porch.

GELLHORN

I'm afraid to ask.

Scared off whoever it was.

MANUEL comes back and stands at the front of the porch steps.

MANUEL

It worked well, Ernesto.

HEMINGWAY

Yes, Manuel, it did. But they'll be back tomorrow.

GELLHORN

I won't.

GELLHORN turns and goes back into the house.

CASEY

I'm beginning to see what you mean about women, Ern.

HEMINGWAY stands and leans the shotgun against the chair.

HEMINGWAY

Case, what would you say to our sparring a few rounds?

Sure, but let's have a drink first.

(They all go into the house.)

⁓

SCENE FIVE

*HEMINGWAY stands alone on the porch.
It is just before dawn. The light advances
incrementally as he speaks.*

HEMINGWAY

I know you're out there, all of you, waiting for me to make a wrong move. Well, keep waiting you sons of whores, you won't get the drop on me. You don't have the guts of the New York critics. At least we know their names. My consolation is that those names will pass from memory faster than a summer squall peters out on Lake Tanganyika.

You think you're not alone in your enterprise, but you are, we all are. Morning, however, is not the time to stab at being profound. No matter what or how well we write or play baseball the light of the world puts every one of us to shame. We humans are all assassins, anyway, and only the very best among us save our bravest act for last. As God is my witness, He witnesses also for Martha and Manuel and Case and Hig, and I am here this beautiful fucking new day to testify that only God can get Ducky Medwick out.

END

KEROUAC
(stops a passing waiter)
Hey, isn't that Crazy Joe Gallo, the gangster, sitting over there?

WAITER
Yeah, but he don't like nobody callin' him crazy. The Columbos hung that on him.

> *JK knocks back a shot of whiskey, puts the glass down on the bar and carries his beer over to GALLO's table. JK stands in front of GALLO, weaving a little, obviously unsteady on his feet. GALLO keeps eating.*

KEROUAC
Mr. Gallo, my name is Kerouac. You may have heard of me. I'm a famous writer.

GALLO looks up at KEROUAC.

GALLO

I read *On the Road*. I liked it, especially the part with the Mexican chick in the dumpy hotel room in L.A. throwin' shoes at Sal. Rang true. I didn't like your next one, though. Too much weird religious stuff in it.

KEROUAC

The Dharma Bums. I'm a Buddhist.

GALLO

Sit down before you fall down.

KEROUAC sits down in a chair opposite GALLO.

KEROUAC

Aren't you afraid to be in here alone?

GALLO

I ain't afraid of nothin'. You know who I am, huh?

KEROUAC

Sure, Crazy Joe Gallo.

GALLO

Call me Joey. I ain't crazy.

KEROUAC

That's what Melville said.

GALLO

Guy who wrote *Moby Dick*?

KEROUAC

He wrote that in a letter to Nathaniel Hawthorne in defense of his novel. Nobody understood it.

GALLO
(laughs)
Some people don't understand me, either. They call me crazy 'cause I take chances, only I don't, really. I know what I'm doin', keepin' people on their toes so's they don't take advantage. Know what I mean, Kerroway?

KEROUAC

Kero-wack. I'm French-Canadian. Iroquois, actually. You read a lot, huh?

GALLO

You think tough guys can't read? I'm thinkin' about writin' a book someday. I'm too busy now. If I ever hafta do hard time, I'll do it.

KEROUAC

Dostoyevsky wrote *The House of the Dead* about his prison experience.

GALLO

Don't know that one. Tried *Crime and Punishment* but I never finished it. Lost interest when the guy lets his conscience bother him. You can't have a conscience in my business. A man does what he's gotta do just to stay in business. Know what I mean? You ever been inside?

KEROUAC

I got married in The Tombs.

GALLO

(stops eating for a moment)

No joke? How'd that happen?

KEROUAC

Got arrested for being an accessory after a crime. The judge let me marry my girlfriend, who was in college. Helped me get off.

GALLO

What was the beef?

KEROUAC

Murder.

GALLO

Christ, Kerroway, you're a reg'lar Dostoyoosky yourself. What an experience.

KEROUAC

Know what Oscar Wilde called experience?

GALLO

Tell me.

KEROUAC

Mistakes.

GALLO

He wasn't half wrong.

KEROUAC

You think intellectuals can't have real life experience? I was a football player, too. Halfback for Columbia until I broke a leg.

The WAITER comes over.

GALLO

Bring this man more of whatever he's havin', and another glass of wine for me.
(to Kerouac)
I stay away from the browns. Gives me the shakes.

The WAITER leaves.

KEROUAC

I'm an alcoholic. So was my father.

GALLO

You won't live long, you keep it up. How old are you?

KEROUAC

Forty.

GALLO

I'm thirty-three. You still married?

KEROUAC

Naw. Twice divorced.

GALLO

But you're a Catholic, ain't ya?

KEROUAC

I told you, I'm a Buddhist.

GALLO

Oh, yeah. It's why you wrote a bad book.

KEROUAC

I just published another one, a confessional, like Fitzgerald's *The Crack-Up*, only he didn't live to finish his.

> *The WAITER brings their drinks and goes away. GALLO lifts his glass and toasts KEROUAC.*

GALLO

To your success.

> *KEROUAC raises his whiskey and they clink glasses and drink.*

KEROUAC

You're a swell guy, Joey. I'm glad we met.

GALLO

As the Frenchman said, two ships passin' in the night.

KEROUAC

Dr. Louis-Ferdinand Celine. *Voyage au Bout de la Nuit*. Almost dawn. He'd be pissing into the Seine about now.

GALLO

I got a story you can write.

KEROUAC

Let's hear it. But I need another drink first.

> *GALLO signals to the WAITER, pointing to KEROUAC.*

GALLO

A guy's married, has a couple of kids, but falls in love with another woman, a showgirl, as it happens. He keeps the showgirl on the side but she cheats on him with some mug, so he threatens to kill the mug unless he lays off the girl.

KEROUAC

But the guy's cheating on his wife.

GALLO

That don't matter. He's payin' her bills.

> *The WAITER brings two more whiskeys. KEROUAC gulps one down.*

KEROUAC

Why doesn't he divorce the wife and marry the showgirl?

GALLO

He does. But then he catches the new wife bangin' the same mug. He drills the mug and is about to drill the girl, too, only he can't bring himself to pull the trigger.

KEROUAC

He loves her too much.

GALLO

I suppose. She helps him dump the body into the East River.

KEROUAC

He tosses the gun in after.

GALLO

Right.

KEROUAC

That's why I got arrested, for dropping the knife my friend used to kill someone down a storm drain. So now the guy has to keep her 'cause she's got the goods on him.

GALLO

You got a brain works like Poe's, Kerroway. Right again. But for some reason, she don't do it for him no more.

KEROUAC

He can't make love to her?

GALLO

Not can't, don't want to. He begs the first wife to take him back, but she don't want him, and besides, she's engaged to be married.

KEROUAC

So he gets another girl.

GALLO

He's already got another girl in mind but she won't tumble unless he gets rid of wife number two.

KEROUAC

Who won't give him a divorce, anyway, for obvious reasons, and he can't force her.

GALLO

Yeah, for obvious reasons and some other reasons not so obvious. What does he do?

> *Grayish light streams through the windows. KEROUAC knocks back his last shot, then staggers to his feet.*

KEROUAC

Like the brilliant but demented doctor, he goes off to micturate in the river but stumbles drunkenly as he's pulling out his pecker, falls in and drowns.

GALLO

That's no solution.

KEROUAC

Closure is always a problem, Joey.

GALLO

Lay off the browns, Kerroway, and you'll live to write another day. You're losin' your looks, too.

> KEROUAC gives GALLO a half-wave
> and wobbles away, out of the restaurant.
> The WAITER comes over.

WAITER

Another glass, Mr. Gallo?

GALLO

No, thanks. Just the check.

WAITER

There's no charge, Mr. Gallo.

> GALLO pulls a roll of bills out of one of his
> pockets, peels off a couple and hands them
> to the WAITER.

GALLO

These are for you.

WAITER

Thank you, Mr. Gallo. Will your friend be coming back?

> *GALLO peels off two more bills from his roll and places them in one of the WAIT-ER's hands.*

GALLO

If he does, this should cover him.

WAITER

Certainly.

> *The WAITER walks away. GALLO stands up and faces the audience.*

GALLO

In ten years, at just about this time of the morning, the Columbos are going to gun me down in front of my family, right here in Umberto's Clam House. Kerouac will have drunk himself to death three years before, twelve years after he became a best-selling author. I never wrote a sentence, but I never served one, either. How's that for closure?

END

THE PITH HELMET

B. Traven

John Huston

CAST OF CHARACTERS

B. TRAVEN, aka **HAL CROVES**, writer, a man in his late forties/
early fifties, provenance uncertain, author of many novels,
one of which, *The Treasure of the Sierra Madre*, is about to
be made into a feature film, starring Humphrey Bogart, that
will make Traven's fortune and him world famous.

JOHN HUSTON, Hollywood director and screenwriter (*The
Maltese Falcon*, et al.) set to embark on the making of the
movie based on Traven's novel. Son of the actor Walter
Huston, who will co-star with Bogart (and win an Academy
Award for his performance). John Huston's reputation as a
drinker, brawler and womanizer precedes him.

HUMPHREY BOGART, an actor

SETTING

The year is 1947. Traven and Huston are about to meet for the
first time at the Hotel Reforma in Mexico City. Traven, however,
is masquerading as Traven's "agent," Hal Croves, for reasons
unknown by Huston. The play takes place in the director's hotel
suite.

A knock at the door. JOHN HUSTON, a tall, lanky man in his early thirtiess, opens it.

HUSTON

Ah, Mr. Croves, I presume.

> *TRAVEN/CROVES enters. He is wearing a slightly soiled white sportcoat, white trousers and a beige pith helmet. HUSTON is dressed casually, slacks and open-collared shirt; half an unlit cigar protrudes from one corner of his mouth. TRAVEN/CROVES surveys the front room of the suite, then stands by a window overlooking the Paseo, his eyes inspecting the director.*

HUSTON

I'm quite alone here at the moment, if that's what's worrying you.

TRAVEN/CROVES
(with German accent)

I am not worried, Mr. Huston, just suspicious. There is a difference.

HUSTON

Nothing to be suspicious about, Croves. Would you like a drink?

TRAVEN/CROVES

I never drink when I am negotiating.

HUSTON

It's the lawyers do the negotiating, not us. Have a seat, won't you? I've been looking forward to meeting and having a conversation with you.

> TRAVEN/CROVES *sits down in a chair. HUSTON sits on the couch and pours himself a drink from a bottle of tequila on the coffee table in front of him.*

HUSTON

When in Mexico.
(He takes a sip of tequila.)
Now, Mr. Croves, I've been given to understand that you are an agent for Mr. Traven.

TRAVEN/CROVES

That is correct.

HUSTON

Why don't you take off that pith helmet? There's not much sun in here.

TRAVEN/CROVES

If it is all right with you, I will leave it on for the moment.

HUSTON

When do I get to meet Traven? I've got a few questions to ask him.

TRAVEN/CROVES

You can ask questions of me and I will relate them to Señor Traven. If he wishes to answer your questions, I will deliver his replies.

HUSTON

See here, Croves, I don't work for the FBI. I just want to make a good movie out of Traven's book. I'm here to discuss any concerns he might have regarding how I go about it and to tell him what I have in mind.

TRAVEN/CROVES

Señor Traven has read your screenplay and is quite satisfied that you have made a proper understanding of his novel. He is experienced in these matters, having written several screenplays for films made here in Mexico. As I make clear, it is Señor Traven's request that anything you wish to tell him you will tell me.

> *HUSTON finishes off his drink, then pours himself another.*

HUSTON

Sure you won't have a shot Mr. Croves? This is top-notch tequila, from Guerrero.

TRAVEN/CROVES waves his hand dismissively.

TRAVEN/CROVES

I don't wish to appear impolite or ungrateful, Mr. Huston, but I must decline this aspect of your hospitality.

HUSTON

I like a man who drinks with me. It's a good way to get to know him.

TRAVEN/CROVES

I have no reason to doubt that you are well-acquainted with many men who share your opinion.

HUSTON

Women, too. The trouble with women is that the better they hold their liquor, the better they lie.

TRAVEN/CROVES

Down.

HUSTON

What's that?

TRAVEN/CROVES

Down. They lie down. Is that what you mean, Mr. Huston?

HUSTON laughs.

HUSTON

You're clever, Croves. Is Traven as clever as you?

TRAVEN/CROVES

Señor Traven is a humanitarian. His desire is through his books to reveal the ultimate futility of greed and avarice so that the unnecessary suffering caused by exploitation of the common man shall be eradicated.

HUSTON

Are you sure you won't imbibe, Mr. Croves? It makes the Wobbly credo go down better.

TRAVEN/CROVES shakes his head no.

HUSTON

Let's talk about *Treasure*. The way I see it, it's Howard, the old man, who's at the center of things. He wants to get rich but he's not greedy, nor is Curtin, though Curtin can be manipulated. Dobbs lacks character and the confidence that goes along with it, so he's dangerous. Traven means Howard to keep the peace but only to a point. He's seen enough to know that sometimes the only resolution to a sticky situation comes out of the barrel of a gun, like Goering said about culture. Either that, or to skedaddle while the skedaddling's good.

TRAVEN/CROVES

You make no attempt to disguise your cynicism, Mr. Huston. I like that. And the precise words of Herr Goering, I believe, were, "When I hear the word culture, I reach for my Luger."

HUSTON

Call me, John, please. My father—who, by the way, has agreed to play the role of old Howard, without his false teeth—told me when I was a boy that it was impolite when in civilized company for a man to wear a hat indoors.

TRAVEN/CROVES

Ah, my pith helmet annoys you, does it?

HUSTON

The helmet doesn't annoy me, only your keeping it on while we talk.

TRAVEN/CROVES takes off the pith helmet and places it down on a chair next to his.

HUSTON

Traven's a German, I understand.

TRAVEN/CROVES

He was born in Chicago and is of Norwegian parentage. He has been living in Mexico for many years.

HUSTON

Why?

TRAVEN/CROVES

Have you ever been in Chicago, Mr. Huston?

HUSTON

I have.

TRAVEN/CROVES

Then you know that it gets extremely cold there. Señor Traven prefers the climate in Mexico.

HUSTON

And you, Croves. You speak English with a German accent.

TRAVEN/CROVES

My parents were from a part of Poland that was taken over during the war. They were ethnic Teutons who spoke German in our house. German was my first language.

HUSTON

How did you and Traven become acquainted?

TRAVEN/CROVES

Quite by chance. But this is not the point of our meeting, Mr. Huston. Señor Traven wishes me to be present as an advisor during the filming. I believe this is stipulated in his contract with the Warner brothers. When are you scheduled to begin?

HUSTON

Next week. Most of the principal cast has arrived and we're doing a run-through the day after tomorrow.

TRAVEN/CROVES

Señor Traven is pleased that Gabriel Figueroa will be the cinematographer. I'm sure you know that they have worked together and are close friends.

HUSTON

I do. Well, then, Croves.
                    (HUSTON stands up.)
I think we're finished here. I'll have my assistant contact you about the shooting schedule. Gabe and I are going to Tampico tonight.

> TRAVEN/CROVES rises and shakes hands with HUSTON.

TRAVEN/CROVES

It has been a pleasure to meet you.

HUSTON

Same here. Give Traven my regards. He wrote a great book. I hope my movie will do it justice.

> TRAVEN/CROVES leaves. Huston pours himself another shot of tequila but before he can drink it, there is a knock at the door.

HUSTON

Come in!

> *HUMPHREY BOGART enters, looks around.*

BOGART

Croves gone?

HUSTON

Just now.

> (He drinks the tequila, holds up his glass.)

You want one?

BOGART

Sure, so long as it doesn't cost me anything.

> *HUSTON pours them both drinks. Hands one to Bogart.*

HUSTON

You're already in character.

BOGART

I like Dobbs. He can't hide his real feelings.

HUSTON

The saints be with us.

> (They drink.)

BOGART

So, John, what's the score with Mr. Croves?

HUSTON

He's a Kraut. He's Traven.

BOGART

Yeah? Why the cover?

HUSTON

Maybe we'll find out. He's gonna be on the shoot with us.

BOGART

Oh, that'll be peachy. What if he doesn't like what he sees?

HUSTON

I can't keep him away. It's in his contract.

BOGART

Jack Warner's a fool to allow it.

HUSTON

Don't worry, Figueroa will handle him. And if he can't, I'll flash
my pistola.

BOGART

Ann Sheridan just pulled in.

HUSTON

Where'd they put her?

BOGART

Here, in the Reforma. Across the hall from me.

HUSTON picks up the half-full bottle of tequila and heads for the door.

HUSTON

Let's go welcome her.

BOGART

She never used to be that kind of girl, John.

HUSTON

How long since you've seen her?

BOGART

A couple of years.

HUSTON

Well, Bogey, a lot can happen to change a person in a couple of years.

BOGART

Just let me get out of there before you start waving your pistola around.

HUSTON opens the door and Bogart exits. Before Huston follows suit, something catches his eye: TRAVEN/CROVES's pith helmet, left on the chair. HUSTON goes over, picks it up and places the helmet on his head. He goes out.

END

IXION IN EXILE

Albert Camus.

CAST OF CHARACTERS

ALBERT CAMUS, French writer, forty-six years old, author of *The Stranger,* well-known for his essay opposing capital punishment

PIXIE, a young prostitute

SETTING

A hotel room in New York City, Summer 1959.

PIXIE is sitting on the edge of the bed, putting on her stockings. Other than that, she is naked. CAMUS is lying on the bed, also nude, smoking a cigarette.

PIXIE

I could, I'd pull the fuckin' switch myself. Way that man treated me deserves be electrified twice.

CAMUS

Yes, Pixie, I understand how you feel. But it is the state that is the machinery carrying out the sentence.

PIXIE

You mean it's okay I do it, then? Leave the state out?

CAMUS

No, Pixie. If in the heat of passion such a crime is committed, if in the course, say, of being beaten and in fear of losing one's life, in self-defense a murder is committed, or if it occurs after a long history of such abuse, even psychological abuse, a legitimate case can be made to justify the act. But the state has no right to act as executioner.

PIXIE
(continues getting dressed)

I be happy scorch that motherfucker. I be happy whoever do it, long as Dorsey be dead.

CAMUS
It's tonight he's being executed?

PIXIE
Tonight at midnight.
(She looks at a clock on a bedside table.)
Thirty-two minutes from now. You ready again? Give you a blowjob twenty extra.

CAMUS
No, merci, Pixie. I am quite satisfied.
(He lights another cigarette from the old one.)

PIXIE is finished dressing. She stops at the door and looks over at CAMUS.

PIXIE
You a nice man, Mister Cam-yoo. All Frenchmen ain't so nice, you know.

CAMUS
Thank you, Pixie. I will remember you with affection.

PIXIE

Bye now. Be careful while you in New York. Be rough you not pay attention.

CAMUS

I will. Good night.

PIXIE leaves. CAMUS smokes, then gets up, looks in the mirror over dresser.

CAMUS
(to his reflection in the mirror)

Who are you to tell anyone how to think or feel about anything? You lie to yourself all the time, not only to others. This is why you write your novels and essays, hiding behind Proust's dictum that literature is the finest kind of lying. You cannot stop lying. For you, it is what makes living tolerable. You are foolish to presume to understand Pixie. To attempt to reason with someone you do not understand is not merely arrogant but absurd. This is the disease of Sartre. To go on lying is your only choice, so better to be good at it.

The telephone rings. CAMUS answers it.

CAMUS

Hello.
(pause)

No, he is not here. He never was, he does not exist. My name is Dorsey, will I do?

END

ALGREN'S INFERNO

nelson Algren
1949

CAST OF CHARACTERS

NELSON ALGREN, writer, author of *The Man with the Golden Arm*. He is forty-six years old, having the night before finished writing his novel, *A Walk on the Wild Side*.

DOLORES LONESOME SOUND, fifty-two years old, part African American, part Native American, formerly a drug addict and alcoholic, now pastor of God's Paradise, a storefront church on West Madison Street, the city's Skid Row.

SETTING

Chicago, 1955. Algren and Dolores Lonesome Sound are standing on West Madison in front of God's Paradise. It is late on a winter afternoon; the sky darkens steadily as the pair converse.

NELSON

Dolores, you don't mind, I hope, that I took the title for my new novel from something you said in one of your sermons.

DOLORES

No, child, 'course not. What was it I said?

NELSON

You were talking about your flock, taking in folks who'd been walking on the wild side and were now ready to enter God's Paradise.

DOLORES

Oh, yes. Yes, Nelson, these are the ones got down so low no place left for 'em to go other than in the dirt. People like myself, the way I used to be, not yet gone but forgotten by everyone 'cept the Lord. You go on use the words do they serve a good purpose. Got any loose behavior in it?

NELSON

Not really. Only drinkin', druggin', whorin', fightin', in order to show how without a helping hand individuals come apart.

DOLORES

Adrift and bereft. How do you get those frightened souls down on paper?

NELSON

Pastor Lonesome Sound, I write about what I see, what most novelists ignore, writers who pick at scabs so small they're not worth a whisper. I hear my characters crying in my sleep.

DOLORES

You are a righteous man, Nelson, and you own all the words.

NELSON

Righteous, perhaps, but never sanctimonious. I don't hide from the horror.

DOLORES

No place to hide. You remember Mister Roland Walks Behind Himself, part Pottawotomi like me? He die night before last.

NELSON

Sure, I used to shoot pool with him at Benzinger's.

DOLORES

Couple hoodlums jackrolled him, he fought back and one of 'em cracked open his skull, left him bleed to death in Losers Alley. Officer Muller tol' me this mornin'. Was Miss Twisty discover the body takin' a trick back there.

NELSON

That's what gets me, Dolores, my writing about all the sadness and bad behavior doesn't really do any good. It doesn't change the way people treat each other or move the powers that be to improve lives of the have-nots. At least you give 'em a bowl of tomato soup.

DOLORES

And a friend in Jesus. You a good writer, Nelson?

NELSON

Some of the deep thinkers back East used to think I was pretty good. Nowadays they can't seem to make use of me, so I'm sliding off the map.

DOLORES

Most everyone 'roun' here never been on no map, no direction home and no home to go to even they got the bus fare. You want to come inside, get warm with some soup?

NELSON

No, thank you, Dolores, but my poker cronies are throwing me a little party to celebrate my finishing my novel.

DOLORES

God's Paradise is for one an' all, Nelson, believers and unbelievers both. You take care now.

> *DOLORES turns and goes inside God's Paradise. The stage is now in almost total darkness. NELSON lights a cigarette.*

NELSON

In New Orleans, I met a whore who had tattooed between her belly button and her pussy the words, "Abandon all hope, ye who enter here." She told me she had a degree in European literature from the University of Texas.

The stage goes dark. The last light we see is from the tip of NELSON's cigarette.

END

THE LAST WORDS OF
ARTHUR RIMBAUD

Rimbaud shortly before
his death — after a sketch
by his sister, Isabelle

PLACE: The Hospital of the Immaculate Conception, Marseilles, France.

TIME: November 9, 1891. The day before Rimbaud's death.

ARTHUR RIMBAUD, thirty-seven years old, the poet and adventurer, lies dying in a hospital bed. He drifts in and out of consciousness, delirious with pain. His right leg has been amputated due to a malignancy.

At his beside sits his sister, ISABELLE RIMBAUD, thirty-one years old. The bed is surrounded by candles, flickering in the otherwise darkened room.

ARTHUR

Tell them, tell them . . . say that I am entirely paralyzed, yes, and so I wish to embark early. Please let me know at what time I should be carried on board.

ISABELLE

My poor Arthur, it's impossible for you to travel. You can't be moved.

ARTHUR

I'll return to Harar, to Djami, he'll be waiting. I'll return with limbs of steel, dark skin and furious eyes. With this mask, people will think I am of a strong race.

ISABELLE

Forget Djami, forget him. I'm here, Isabelle, your sister. Think of me, of our mother, the ones who love you most.

ARTHUR

My name carved in stone at Luxor, only the wind and sand can erase it. Tell Djami I am coming, I will see him again soon. My one friend, my only friend.

ISABELLE

Djami cannot help you, Arthur. That boy is far from here, in Abyssinia. Probably dead.

ARTHUR

Send him money, three thousand francs. Tell him his master, who loves him, begs he make wise use of this sum, that he invest it prudently in an enterprise sure to realize a profit. Tell him not to be idle. His wife and child must prosper.

ISABELLE

Arthur, pray. Forget Africa.

ARTHUR

Djami and I . . . two ghosts . . . slipping through the subtle air. Sons of the sun.

Writers

ISABELLE

All the years away from France, broiling in the heat, your brain was affected.

ARTHUR

Capsule rifles, two thousand-forty at fifteen Marie Thérèse dollars each. Sixty thousand Remington cartridges at sixty dollars the thousand. Tools of various kinds valued at five thousand-eight hundred dollars. Total value of caravan forty thousand. Fifty days to Menelek, king to pay us on arrival. We leave from Tadjoura. Ivory, musk, gold. The Choans would have our testicles! French testicles. Harar to Antotto, twenty days. Avoid Dankalis, evil savages. Sixty thousand dollars, exchange at Aden, 4.3 francs, equals 258,000 francs. Coffee or slaves. Won't take Egyptian piasters. Caravans form at Djibouti. Did I marry the Somali girl? She went back, Djami sent her away. Not my orders. Find Djami, quick! My leg, must rest my leg before meeting the Emir. Turks and cannons.

ISABELLE

(praying)

Oh Lord, I weep! Lord, soften his agony. Help him to bear his cross. Have pity on my brother, his poor soul that writhes on earth. Have pity and take him, oh Lord. You who are so good, so kind.

ARTHUR

The hyenas laugh at us. Their laughing keeps me awake. Smelling my wound. Poetry poured from the open wound, words spilled until there was nothing left. Emptied, I fled. Djami, your warmth. She is far off, master, to BarAbir. Far, far. Cannot go there with accounts due. The business. Cheated by Menelek, cunning, cunning. Le Bosphore Egyptien, my case. Ragged, dirty rags, no way for a French citizen. Dead before my time, the late Arthur Rimbaud. I have been bitten by life before and survived. Two terrible years and nothing to show.

ISABELLE

Arthur, do you know me? Do you know your sister, your youngest sister, Isabelle? Can you feel my strength, my love? The love of the Lord that flows through me.

ARTHUR

I see you, my angel. My angel of happiness.

ISABELLE

Oh, yes! Yes, Arthur! I am! Your angel. Oh, thank you, Lord, for bringing my brother home before . . . before. . . .

ARTHUR

Before his death. The death of the late Arthur Rimbaud.

ISABELLE

No, perhaps it is possible that you may live! The Lord is merciful, it's in His power to heal.

ARTHUR

We'll walk then, you and I, around Harar, when my new leg is attached, my artificial limb. You won't believe the colors! And Aden, we'll journey to Aden. I can arrange things there, arms for the South. Tell Djami, my man, my one brother under the sun, I am on my way! I'm coming with snow on my scarf, flowers from the Ardennes, things he's never seen! Wake me before the harbor burns. It will burn after our boat departs, so we can watch the flames from the deck as we disappear over the horizon, a spectacle of fire, our farewell.

ISABELLE

Arthur, Arthur! Are you gone?

ARTHUR

Sails . . . yellow, red . . . the sea.

END

SERIOUS ENOUGH

Jane Bowles

Certainly I am nearer to becoming
a saint ...

CAST OF CHARACTERS

JANE BOWLES, forty-five years old, author of the novel *Two Serious Ladies* and a play, *In the Summer House*

BRENDA, well-dressed woman in late middle age

BARTENDER

A MAN

SETTING

The bar of the Stanhope Hotel in New York City, December 1962.

JANE BOWLES enters the elegantly appointed bar and takes a seat. The Stanhope is a first-class hotel. She takes off her gloves, unfastens her coat and removes her hat, revealing unruly dark hair, cut short. She shivers from the cold. Seated a couple of stools away is BRENDA, smoking a cigarette in a long holder and sipping a martini. They are the only two customers in the bar on a mid-afternoon. The BARTENDER comes over to JANE.

BARTENDER

May I serve you, madam?

JANE

I suppose, yes.

(points to Brenda's glass)

What is she drinking?

BARTENDER

A Beefeater martini, straight up, two olives.

JANE hesitates.

BARTENDER

English gin. Very dry.

JANE

Fine, I'll have that.

> *The BARTENDER walks away.*

JANE
(to BRENDA)

Hi, my name is Jane.

BRENDA

Mine is Brenda.

JANE
(still shivering)

I'm not used to the cold any more. I grew up here but I haven't been in New York for two years.

BRENDA

Do you live in Florida?

JANE

Oh, no, Florida is a terrible place. My mother lives there. I live in Tangier, Morocco.

BRENDA

You're a long way from home. I've never been to North Africa. What do you do there?

JANE

Oh, I write, and mingle with the natives. My husband writes, too, and he composes music. We're in New York now because he has a job composing music for a Broadway play. His name is Paul. My mother and sister were just here, from Florida, to visit me. They left this morning, thank goodness. We don't get on well together, not well at all. Is your mother still alive?

BRENDA

No.

JANE

That's one less thing you have to worry about.

The BARTENDER brings Jane her drink.

BARTENDER

One Beefeater martini, straight up, two olives.

He walks away. JANE lifts the glass to her lips.

BRENDA

Don't drink it too fast. It's very cold.

JANE

Thanks for the tip.

She sips tentatively.

JANE

Ooh, you're right.

(shivers again)

BRENDA

What sort of writing do you do, Jane?

JANE

Short stories, a play. Now I'm trying to write a novel.

BRENDA

Do you have a title? I often buy a book just because I like the title.

JANE

Three Serious Ladies, or maybe it's only *Two Serious Ladies*. I haven't decided yet. Is it good for you, Brenda? The title, I mean. Would it appeal to you enough to make you want to buy it?

BRENDA

I'm not sure. Perhaps, if the cover art attracted me. How serious are these two or three ladies?

JANE

Serious enough. Each of them is searching for the best way to live her life. And with whom, if there is a whom. Where do you live?

BRENDA

Aren't we all. I live here, in the Stanhope.

JANE

I like to come in here when I'm in New York. Charlie Parker died in this hotel. Did you know that ? In a suite occupied by a very rich heiress.

BRENDA

The Baroness. Yes, I knew her. She moved to New Jersey after that musician died.

JANE

He and his friend Dizzy Gillespie invented bop. Do you like jazz? My husband hates it. Oh, I'm sorry, asking you all these questions.

BRENDA

Drink your martini, Jane. You don't want it to cool down too much.

> JANE and BRENDA both sip from their
> glasses.

JANE

Do you prefer women or men, Brenda? To sleep with.

BRENDA
(laughs)

I sleep with Horatio. He's been fixed.

JANE stares at her.

BRENDA

My poodle.

BRENDA signals to the bartender, who comes over and presents BRENDA with a check, which she signs, then stands up. The BAR-TENDER picks up the check and moves away.

BRENDA

It's been interesting talking with you, Jane. I'll look for your novel.

JANE

Oh, it'll be a while before it's published. That's if I can find a publisher for it, of course. Only one other person has read what I've written so far and he said it was unrelievedly unorthodox.

BRENDA

How could it be otherwise? Good luck, Jane.

BRENDA leaves the bar. JANE watches her go, then looks around nervously before lifting her glass and swallowing the remainder of her martini all at once.

JANE

Bartender! Oh, bartender!

He comes over.

JANE

Are there many women living alone in this hotel?

BARTENDER

A few. Would you like another martini?

JANE

I have an appointment with a psychiatrist this afternoon. Do you think I should?

BARTENDER

That's not for me to say, madam.

JANE

I'm not a really serious drinker. I'll bet you know if someone is a serious drinker or not as soon as they sit down at the bar, don't you?

A MAN enters and takes a seat at the oppo-site end of the bar.

BARTENDER
(to JANE)

Pardon me, madam. I'll come back.

He walks away to wait on the man. Jane puts on her gloves, removes an olive from her glass and eats it, then does the same with the other olive. She puts on her hat.

JANE

If I can't take myself seriously, why should I expect anyone else to?

She picks up her glass and holds it out in front of her.

JANE

Bartender! A martini, please, straight up, two olives!

END

THE CAPTIVE

Proust on his deathbed

CAST OF CHARACTERS

MARCEL PROUST, writer, author of the monumental novel *À la recherche du temps perdu* (*In Search of Lost Time*)

THE ANGEL OF DEATH, female, wearing a black cape and cowl

SETTING

The bedroom of Marcel Proust, Paris, France, 1922. He is lying on what will very soon be his deathbed. The furnishings are sumptuous albeit stuffy, overly done; a claustrophobic atmosphere.

PROUST is on the bed surrounded by the scattered printer's page proofs of his massive novel. He is revising the volume entitled La prisonnière *(*The Captive*).*

PROUST

Oh, the agony! It's bad enough to know that I'm about to die, but worse to realize that my book will never be properly finished. I'm barely able to breathe and here I am mincing my words—Albertine's words—regarding anal intercourse. Of course she must be made to make reference to it obliquely, even reluctantly. She cannot be allowed to say it straight out, "me faire casser le pot." Not even the boys in my hotel would use such a term. No, she must let the word "asshole" slip out, as if she is perhaps conversing with one of her girlfriends, and immediately be ashamed for having even referred to the act in my—the narrator's—presence. Here, I'll fix it.

PROUST crosses out words on the page in front of him, writes in others.

There, done! I suppose I'll be dead and never know if even this sanitized sentence survives.

The door to the bedroom flies open and there appears in the doorway THE ANGEL OF DEATH. A female of indeterminate age, she spreads the folds of her great cape like a peacock displaying its wings and tail. PROUST looks up from his manuscript and sees her.

PROUST

No, no, not yet! I've not finished revising my masterpiece.

ANGEL

(advancing toward the bed)

Don't insult my intelligence, Marcel. Your masterpiece, you call it. Scribbling about ass-fucking. Forcing Albertine to speak of your favorite activity, bending over to accommodate the stiffened members of street boys.

PROUST

They were always well paid! None ever complained.

ANGEL

What about ordering them to pierce live rats with hatpins while you watched and masturbated?

PROUST

If anyone refused to do so, they weren't forced.

ANGEL

They weren't paid, then, either. Nor invited back.

PROUST

Why pay someone for what he wouldn't do?

ANGEL

I suppose you expect to go to heaven?

PROUST

If there were such a place, no doubt it would be restricted.

ANGEL

If indeed there were such places as heaven and hell your being a Jew would not determine your fate. You're a captive of your own devices.

PROUST

Leave me be, can't you? I want to get this right. The novel is all I have to leave for posterity.

ANGEL

You and I both know that you've never had any intention of completing it.

PROUST

I want it to be perfect. Is that too much to ask?

ANGEL

Yes, it is.

PROUST writes a bit more, then lays down his pen, rests his head back on his pillows, and closes his eyes.

PROUST

I've always thought an exception would be made in my case.

The ANGEL covers PROUST with her cape.

END

THE TRUE TEST OF GREATNESS

melville

CAST OF CHARACTERS

HERMAN MELVILLE, author of *Moby Dick*, *Billy Budd*, and
other books

A POLICEMAN

SETTING

Melville is walking on a dock along the waterfront in New York
City on October 18, 1888. Night has fallen. He stops and looks
out over the Hudson River. Melville is wearing a long overcoat and
a hat. A uniformed policeman approaches him.

POLICEMAN

Out for a stroll, are we?

MELVILLE

I'm just off work. Looking at the river helps me clear my head.

POLICEMAN

Where do you work?

MELVILLE

At the Customs House. I'm a clerk there.

POLICEMAN

I don't think I'd like bein' cooped up inside an office all day long. I'd rather be walkin' a beat.

MELVILLE

I wasn't always at a desk. Before I was a writer, I was a merchant seaman.

POLICEMAN

A writer? I thought you worked at the Customs House.

MELVILLE

I do. Before that I wrote stories, novels. And before that I went to sea.

POLICEMAN

I'm not much of a reader, except for the newspaper. Wrote anything that was popular?

MELVILLE

Early on, I did. *Omoo*, *Typhoo*. As long as I kept to tales of adventure, I did right well, made a good living, good enough to support my family. Then I made the mistake of a lifetime.

POLICEMAN

You didn't kill nobody, I hope.

MELVILLE

I did. Thirty-seven years ago today, on October 18, 1851, I murdered Herman Melville.

POLICEMAN

Who was he?

MELVILLE

The writer I told you about, the author of boys' sea stories.

POLICEMAN

Come again?

MELVILLE

Myself, I murdered myself, in the belief that readers would understand where I was trying to take them. They jumped ship, and the publishers thought I'd gone crazy. So did Hawthorne.

POLICEMAN

Is that why you're workin' down here now?

MELVILLE

Better the Customs House than the poorhouse.

POLICEMAN

It's no crime to be doin' government work. Right honorable, in fact.

MELVILLE

In some men's eyes, honor alone might amount to a criminal condition.

POLICEMAN

I don't know as I can rightly judge your meanin', sir.

MELVILLE

That's at the heart of it, officer. Meaning depends upon whoever's doing the judging.

POLICEMAN

I'd better be makin' my way along now. You wouldn't be thinkin' of doin' anything foolish, would you?

MELVILLE

Though I am sleepy, I dare not. If there is one thing that I have learned, it's that there is more power and beauty in the well-kept secret of one's self and one's thoughts than in the display of a whole heaven that one may have inside him.

POLICEMAN
I'll be saying good evenin', then, sir.

The POLICEMAN walks away.

MELVILLE
(to the river)
Until the oozy weeds about me twist, I'll say it: I ain't crazy.

END

FAREWELL LETTER

Baudelaire at the
Hôtel Lauzun

Jeanne Duval
after Baudelaire
by BG 23.11.84

CAST OF CHARACTERS

CHARLES BAUDELAIRE, French poet, most famously author
   of *Les Fleurs du Mal*. He is twenty-three years old.

THE VOICE OF JEANNE DUVAL, an actress

SETTING

Baudelaire's atelier, Paris, 1844

BAUDELAIRE enters his apartment, sees a letter addressed to him that has been slipped under his door. He picks it up, opens the envelope, removes the missive and sits down at his table. As he reads, we hear THE VOICE OF JEANNE DUVAL reciting the contents of the letter.

THE VOICE OF JEANNE DUVAL

Charles, from the beginning you always
made me laugh. Sending flowers to my
dressing room at Le Théâtre du Panthéon as if
I were a real actress
not just a piece of fluff
trotted out for a few moments in a brief
costume
to make the boys' cocks hard.
You had money, you were charming
and respectful. You appeared impervious to

the fact of my blackness.
When we entered a café together
you were like a proud buck with his doe. All
eyes were on us as we paraded through, and
you treated me as if I were a great lady; you
had the finest manners.
The apartment you bought for me was
furnished exquisitely.
It resembled a Kaliph's boudoir. If only you
had been a Kaliph!
That would have made my being a whore
more palatable. Expensive whores
live longer that the rest.
Nadar knew me before you, yes, as did
Banville.
When you first brought me to your suite at
the Hôtel Lauzun I pretended
never to have been there before.
But I had, several times, with different men,
men who knew how to satisfy a woman,
and themselves.
You created me for yourself as an object only,
a stone creature whom you could idealize
and pretend to worship and torture yourself
over. It was madness!
I'm a slut, yes, perhaps worse; a drunkard,
too. But I am real! I exist here in this time,
not in any other and I never will.
Your reliance on women such as Luchette
and Madame Meurice has stunted you.
They encourage your impotence.
"My vampire!" you called me. It's what you
wanted, begged for, demanded.

Only by cruelty could you be convinced of
anything. Being cruel is
a soul-consuming task, and one which
amuses me to a lesser degree than you
would suppose.
I plead exhaustion, Charles.
I release myself from this obligation to you.
My sweet, poetry is not enough.

Jeanne

*BAUDELAIRE lays the letter down on his
table.*

BAUDELAIRE

So, I achieve what I deserve. The petals part
to reveal the flower of evil. It's what I was
after all along, of course,
a cause to vent my premature spleen.
O, Death, old captain, shall I waste
my breath before our time to meet arrives?
What better to do but spit beauty at despair?

END

THE NOBODY

Emily Dickinson

CAST OF CHARACTERS

EMILY DICKINSON, fifty-one years old, an unpublished poet

LAVINIA, her sister

SETTING

The parlor of the Dickinson family, Amherst, Massachusetts, in 1882. The two sisters are seated at a table, drinking tea.

LAVINIA

Perhaps we'll be able now to become closer.

EMILY

What do you mean by "now"?

LAVINIA

Now that Mother is gone and we're living together.

EMILY

The one has nothing to do with the other.

LAVINIA

After all, we are sisters.

EMILY

Please, Lavinia. Why this sudden desire?

LAVINIA

But I love you, Emily.

EMILY

The test of love, Lavinia, is death.

LAVINIA

Why be rude? I'm trying . . .

EMILY

Don't try.

LAVINIA

You were nice to me once, before you visited Father in Washington, when he was in Congress. After that, after your . . . interlude in Philadelphia, you were different.

EMILY

I was twenty-three.

LAVINIA

Thirty years ago.

EMILY

Twenty-eight.

LAVINIA

Can't you tell me about him now, Emily? What really did happen? He was a poet, too, wasn't he? I know he was a preacher, and married.

EMILY

From whom do you get this information?

LAVINIA

About him, from Susan. About you, my own experience.

EMILY

Our sister-in-law was earlier capable of keeping a confidence. No longer does her heart control her mind. Her mind controls her heart.

Writers

LAVINIA

She and Austin both care about your welfare.

EMILY

Why? I'm nobody. Who are you? Aren't you nobody, too?

LAVINIA

You're afraid to think about it, aren't you? The moment that changed your life.

EMILY

Do you suppose I could be she? This person you imagine me to be?

LAVINIA

I am waiting for her to reveal herself.

EMILY

All things come to she who waits. Alas, come they not 'til past the pearly gates.

LAVINIA

You remain inscrutable.

EMILY

What would please you most, Lavinia? To know if at the age of twenty-three I allowed an older, married man—a minister—to deflower me?

LAVINIA

You do write often of flowers.

EMILY

And since a score and eight I've had no bread upon my plate.

EMILY stands, begins to walk, then collapses to the floor. LAVINIA rushes to her and kneels at EMILY's side.

LAVINIA

Forgive me, sister. I'll not mention this again.

EMILY

Oh, Lavinia, it does not matter. Nothing happened to me, that's what happened.

EMILY rises to her feet. LAVINIA stands next to her.

LAVINIA

Nor to me. We are fortunate, Emily, aren't we? To have avoided everything?

EMILY

There is nothing less, Lavinia, and as we know it to be true, nothing less will do.

They embrace.

END

Writer

AFTER WORDS

Borges

Roberto Bolaño

CAST OF CHARACTERS

JORGE LUIS BORGES, during his lifetime (1899–1986) an Argentinian writer, now a ghost

ROBERTO BOLAÑO, a Chilean writer living in Spain, forty-nine years old

SETTING

Bolaño is walking along the beach near his residence in Blanes, Spain, in 2001. He is smoking a cigarette. He stops when he hears a voice behind him.

BORGES

I've been given to understand that you are, in a literary way, impersonating me.

> BOLAÑO *turns around and sees the ghost*
> *of JORGE LUIS BORGES.*

BOLAÑO

This can't be. You're dead.

BORGES

So will you be. Quite soon, as the doctors have informed you. That's why I've chosen this moment to confront you, while you still have time to admit it.

BOLAÑO

You could have waited, couldn't you? When both of us were ghosts.

BORGES

You don't know how difficult it can be to locate a fellow shade.

I've been searching for Melville for years without success. But tell me, is this compulsion of yours an homage or are you feeding off my corpus?

BOLAÑO

Clever of you to make the distinction between corpus and corpse. Your body of work as opposed to your body.

BORGES

Hardly. I was never lazy when it came to knowing the correct words. They were the missiles in my arsenal.

BOLAÑO

I assume you're referring to my story, "The Insufferable Gaucho." If not for "The South," which you singled out as your favorite among your own stories, there would be no modern Latin American literature.

BORGES

I immodestly concur.
                    (He bows slightly.)

BOLAÑO

I honor you each time I pick up a pen. I like the idea of your looking over my shoulder. In fact, I wouldn't mind your admonishing me whenever you see where I'm going wrong.

BORGES

I'm blind, Bolaño. I can't tell what you're writing. It's only well after the fact, when a friendly familiar reads to me from a book or newspaper, that I'm able to make a judgment. My methods affect your essays as well as your stories.

BOLAÑO

Señor Borges, my intentions are honorable, I assure you. I've written badly at times, of course. Not so badly at others. I'm sloppy sometimes, repetitious, self-indulgent, ignorant, even mean-spirited. After all, I have to make a living. I have a wife and two children to support.

BORGES

I like what you've written about Turgenev. I encountered him not long after my death. He told me he was especially fond of my story, "Funes, the Memorius," and invited me to join the Russian and French writers in their nightly game of pinochle. Of course I declined, but I did compose a story in my mind involving an unrequited love affair between the queen of spades and the knave of diamonds, which ended badly. Pinochle is interesting in principle if only for the exclusive use of cards above the number eight, which is the sign for infinity set vertically.

BOLAÑO

Did you return Turgenev's compliment?

BORGES

I said I thought he'd missed the mark with *Rudin*.

BOLAÑO

I agree, but he was young when he wrote it, he didn't know enough of life yet. I've always thought it could have been made into a good movie. It still could, though Hollywood would have the woman he spurned witness his death on the barricades.

BORGES

Due to my condition, I've no use for the cinema.

BOLAÑO

It was good of Hemingway to list *The Sportsman's Notebook* as one of his foundation texts. Also *Fathers and Sons*. He took that title for one of his own short stories.

BORGES

I've forgotten everything of Hemingway's except for "The Undefeated," the one about Manuel Garcia, a forlorn and doomed old matador. When finally the sword found its way, Manuel Garcia buried four fingers and his thumb into the bull. Badly gored, he needed to mix his own blood with that of his adversary's. Hemingway was only in his twenties when he wrote that story, yet it's very wise.

BOLAÑO

It's fashionable these days to bash Hemingway. I admire him for giving credit to his most significant influences. Camus took his style from Hemingway and James M. Cain.

BORGES

You're cheeky, but serious, Bolaño, a mildly entertaining and very bad critic. Come find me after your death. We'll have plenty of time to talk.

BOLAÑO

How do I find you? You haven't yet come across Melville though you've been dead for years.

BORGES

It will happen eventually. There's a great deal of traffic in these corridors. Perhaps he doesn't want to talk. I've heard he's still bitter about not having been able to publish his masterpiece, *Billy Budd*, during his lifetime. You and I are bound to collide sooner or later. When we do, I'll tell you what's missing in your work.

BOLAÑO

What's missing? Why not tell me now, while I'm still writing?

BORGES

Go again to "The South." Therein lies the key.

*JORGE LUIS BORGES disappears.
ROBERTO BOLAÑO looks in every
direction but the ghost is gone.*

BOLAÑO

Damn, I hate mysteries! This is a story I could have written, one without an answer. Only Borges could have written it better.

END

MUSIC

James Joyce

Samuel Beckett

CAST OF CHARACTERS

JAMES JOYCE, Irish writer, author of *Ulysses* and *Finnegans Wake*

SAMUEL BECKETT, Irish writer, author of the plays *Waiting for Godot* and *Krapp's Last Tape*, among many others. At this time he is Joyce's secretary.

SETTING

The study in the Joyce family apartment, Paris, France, 1921. Joyce and Beckett are seated across the room from one another in armchairs. Joyce is reading a book; Beckett sits with a notebook and pen, waiting.

THE PLAY

For ten minutes the only sound is that of JOYCE murmuring occasionally and turning the pages of his book. Finally, JOYCE speaks.

JOYCE

Music!

BECKETT writes the word in his notebook, after which both men are silent for an indeterminate time, until

END

ABOUT BARRY GIFFORD

Barry Gifford's fiction, nonfiction and poetry have been published in twenty-eight languages. His novel *Night People* was awarded the Premio Brancati, established by Pier Paolo Pasolini and Alberto Moravia, in Italy, and he has been the recipient of awards from PEN, the National Endowment for the Arts, the American Library Association, the Writers Guild of America, and the Christopher Isherwood Foundation. His books *Sailor's Holiday* and *The Phantom Father* were each named a Notable Book of the Year by the *New York Times*, and his book *Wyoming* was named a Novel of the Year by the *Los Angeles Times*. He has written librettos for operas by the composers Toru Takemitsu, Ichiro Nodaira, and Olga Neuwirth. Gifford's work has appeared in many publications, including *The New Yorker, Punch, Esquire, La Nouvelle Revue Française, El País, La Repubblica, Rolling Stone, Brick, Film Comment, El Universal, Projections*, and the *New York Times*. His film credits include *Wild at Heart, Perdita Durango, Lost Highway, City of Ghosts, Ball Lightning, American Falls*, and *The Phantom Father*. Barry Gifford's most recent books are *Sailor & Lula: The Complete Novels, Sad Stories of the Death of Kings, Imagining Paradise: New & Selected Poems, The Roy Stories*, and *The Up-Down*. He lives in the San Francisco Bay Area. For more information visit www.BarryGifford.com.